Life of Clouds

Life of Clouds

by

Noreen Lace

Life of Clouds

Editor: Della Rey
Art Direction: SunBow Productions

ISBN:9780692744758
Library of Congress Control Number: 2016945183
REaDLips Press
Los Angeles, California
2016

For the truest loves of my life, my daughters.
Life didn't exist before you;
With you,
came foundation and form,
beauty and purpose.
With you,
the creation of the deepest love
a person could ever know.

The Cloud People

My dear, there is nothing to be afraid of. In the sky are cloud people. Cloud people have big families who hold grand parties. At these parties, they dance. When they dance, they jump and laugh. When they jump, the sky grows dark. When they laugh, the sky rumbles. Sometimes they jump and laugh so hard the sound rumbles through the darkened skies for all to hear.

Chloe, The House's Wife

My sister, a long time ago, wished her life away. Chloe'd wake early every morning, tired from lack of sleep, dress, style her hair, put make up on, then lie back down desiring the day to pass, quicken the night to fall down upon her and end the day. She lived many lifetimes like this, wishing her life away.

One day, she didn't get out of bed at all. Stayed in her men's flannel pj bottoms bought from Sears as a Christmas gift by her mother the year before and a once white t-shirt that'd turned a dingy shade of dirty dishwater from age, wear, and lack of washing. She remained in her little abode, a dank place on the corner of W. 101st and Lakewood Avenue, and for a long time didn't attempt the day, not for the phone, not for the television; only when hunger threatened to drive her mad, she climbed out of bed to make tea. She sat on the arm of the couch, rocked gently back and forth, back and forth, sipped green tea and nibbled, much like a mouse, on the tea cookies found in the kitchen cabinet. For some length of time, she stared at a blank television screen. As she sat on the corner of her couch, nibbled on the corner of the cookie, she looked up at the ceiling for no apparent reason. Her gaze followed the moldings around the room, down to the baseboards; she jumped off the sofa and pulled it away from the wall. What she saw horrified her, sent a chill down through the front of her chest; she shuddered, made little noises. In a frenzy, she searched her kitchen cabinets for cleaning solution and rags. So completely disgusted at the dust collected all about the furniture and television, she began at the baseboards, scrubbed them clean inching her way around the room.

"How could I not notice this?"

Anything found on the floor that day, and the days after, anything found behind the furniture as well, was thoroughly wrapped in a plastic Safeway supermarket bag and tossed into the garbage. She scrubbed the back of the television. Unplugged all connections prior to cleaning, started to reconnect them, but thought a drip could cause a spark that'd kill her and the whole neighborhood. She cleaned the walls, went down to the basement for a stepladder, continued her binge upon the ceiling. Hours later, she moved the furniture back into place and, horrified by the dust on her hands from the furniture itself, the bookshelf especially, she flung all the items, books, pictures, knick-knacks to the floor and scrounged for more clean dusting rags, more cleaner. With a torn up t-shirt and a can of Pledge found in the back of one of the cabinets, she began to dust the bookshelf, the books, the covers, the spine, the inside front cover, the inside back cover, the page edges. Chloe believed the dust caused the tiredness that'd sunk into her bones.

The moon rose to announce midnight by the time she'd cleaned all she could clean in that room. She walked through the five-room apartment resolute she'd have to clean each of the rooms thoroughly, including the hallway and the closet. Before falling into bed that night, she ran a bath, soaked in it for more than an hour, soaping, rinsing, resoaping, letting the water out, putting more in, washed again. Somewhere between two and five, Chloe fell into a dream wherein dust molecules floated above her like stars, forcing their way into her nostrils, her mouth; she choked awake, laid on the sofa until the first misty rays of daylight flickered through the curtains.

"The curtains!" She gasped, jumped up, and ripped them down. That day, she moved onto the next room.

That is how she lived. She scrubbed, drank tea, ate tea cookies until she ran out of those. Her mother brought groceries. Chloe both liked and disliked Mother's visits. While Chloe couldn't stand to have company any more, the food refreshed her state of mind. Sometimes, her mother didn't bring her the correct food, she'd "try new things" that Chloe had no desire to try. She'd sit helplessly on the cold plastic kitchen chair and cry as, the whole time, her mother repeated unhelpful things.

"If you would just go get some fresh air."

Her family thought the cleaning obsession a little overboard. Her mother'd never kept such a spotless house and none of her children died or got sick from it. Her family also believed her lazy.

"If you want to be a house wife, you need to find a husband," Mother offered.

"If she had children to take up the hours," Grandmother weighed in, "she'd not be focused on useless tasks.

For more than a year she did not leave her apartment, not to the store, the mall, or out with friends. The hours she didn't spend cleaning, she sat on the edge of her couch, nibbled on the corner of a cookie, rocked ever slowly back and forth, back and forth.

Unemployment supported her before she applied for disability, citing her inability to leave the house as a handicap.

"You're going to have to see a doctor," the underpaid civil servant on the other end of the phone sighed.

"No, no, you don't understand. I cannot leave. If I walk out on my patio, I will die."

The search for a house-calling doctor strained her frazzled nerves. This is the city; this is the twentieth-first century; doctors didn't make house-calls. Three long, horrifying attempts, family members urged her on, held her hand, put her into the car. Warned ahead of time, the nurses helped, prepared, rushed her through the backdoor where the doctor's nurses looked at her. Sympathy waned, they were overwhelmed by what she expected from them, even though they'd been forewarned. After her panic attack in front of other patients, they put her in a room to wait for the doctor. While alone in the room, she inspected the cleanliness of the office, found it to be subpar. Her heart pounded, skipped beats, forehead began to sweat, her throat, she was certain, started closing.

By the time the doctor arrived, she stood over the examining table holding her chest, forcing air in and out of her lungs. The doctor, unaware of her condition because he'd barely glanced at the chart, thought it was a heart attack, put on his stethoscope at once and went to her to listen. But he could hear nothing abnormal.

"What seems to be the problem?"

"I can't breathe."

He listened to her lungs.

"I'm tired all the time."

"Do you get enough sleep? Enough food? Enough exercise?"

Although the answers to all were truly no, she nodded thinking the opposite to be true.

"I'm not finding anything physically wrong with you. I am going to order blood tests."

"Blood tests? No." The thought of needles sent her into hysterical sobs.

The older doctor, stooped when he walked, looked at her in a puzzled manner. Everything, he believed, could be explained by medical science. Blood tests were needed to determine the deficiency which had sent her into this physical or psychological decline.

"Can you fill out this paper for disability?"

He nodded. Not that he would fill out the paper, but now he understood. "Not without blood tests."

She cried, but consented to the blood tests. He filled out the papers for disability, unfavorably. Although he didn't believe it would help, he suggested a psychological evaluation. To her family, he suggested that they get her out of the house for a walk in the fresh air.

"Get her a cat, for chrissake," he barked.

They gifted her a white kitten.

Ashley, The Warrior Princess

The little red haired sister disappeared a few years before her sweet sixteen. While she might be considered a runaway, that'd carry connotations of someone looking for her or having called the authorities to report such a thing. She was just gone for a while. When she returned, she carried battle wounds, some physically manifested on her arms; fresh as well as old markings that told her family where she'd been, if not the location, then the destination. She offered no explanations, no tales of the wild, just a strange quietness that'd never been part of her personality before.

She'd developed a fear of moving vehicles, couldn't get into a car, truck, or bus of any kind. She no longer strayed very far. When she did want to go anywhere, for groceries or even clothes, she'd walk the whole way there and the whole way back. Some stores she could not venture to, because, as the family later found out, she couldn't walk over, under, or even around bridges. One of the bridges in the area connected over the railroad tracks on 150th street, another was a pedestrian bridge over the freeway, fenced 360 degrees that she'd played on as a child, and then the small bridge that was over the small stream at a park.

Ashley sat in her room, listened to music, told herself her heart still beat and she could control it; the heart wouldn't beat faster than she wanted, nor was it slowing as she feared. Quietly, she counted the beats, check the pocket chart she'd picked up some time ago in a doctor's office. Sometimes her head pounded. Certain she could feel the veins in her head contract and expand, she convinced herself she had an aneurysm. On one such occasion, she ran downstairs to where her grandmother and mother sat and she started screaming uncontrollably.

"Emergency room, take me. I need...."

Grandmother grabbed her purse, jumped in the car, and began to back down the driveway, turn the corner toward the hospital, toward the emergency room, and before they would even come to the bridge, the movement of the car caused Ashley to jump out and run home. The first happening, Grandmother panicked, tried to get her back in the car, but Ashley ran off into the darkness.

Now, used to this, Grandmother agreed to take her to the emergency room, hoped this time they would make it, that this time she'd get her all the way there and the doctors could figure out what was so completely wrong, not these momentary lapses of reason in which she thought she was dying, but everything else too. And now, when Little Red jumped out of the car,

Grandmother slowly followed her home, resigned to the fact that once again they failed and nothing could force her.

They tried once, Grandmother on one side, Mother on the other side, Ashley in the middle, to force her to the hospital, to the doctor, to anywhere that might get her the help she needed, whatever help that might be, or not be. But the girl freaked out, pounded her hands, kicked her feet on the windshield, on them, and they had to let her out barely half way down the block. She ran the whole way back to the house.

Reading was a pastime Ashley no longer enjoyed. If anything happened in the book, the newspaper, or magazine, she would think it might happen to her. Once she read about a woman with breast cancer: she walked around for two days with her hands on her breasts, insisted she felt something like a lump, broke into a crying fit, begged someone, anyone, to drive her to the emergency room. However, the family tired of it, if not the dramatics, then the sheer time and will it took to get her in the car only for her to jump out and run away. She no longer watched television, a shooting, a robbery, or any of the like, convinced the youngest sister the next store patronized would be robbed, the next person who drove by would shoot her down, and that made her unable to venture far from home.

So Ashley spent much time away from the house, away from the television, the newspaper, and from people who talked about those things. Sometimes, she still hid battle wounds.

But she tired of the routine, forced herself to stand at the corner near the bridge and look up at it, to face it down, to tell it that it could not beat her, could not control her, could not keep her from her destination and she did this for some time without much success of getting any closer to approaching or overtaking the bridge. She would sit in Grandma's car for hours at a time, doors open, windows open, attempt to overcome what she thought to be claustrophobia.

She walked to a doctor whose office opened on this side of the bridge. The woman doctor was young and nice. But Ashley was not. So when the woman suggested a psychiatrist, Ashley bit out obscenities at her. After the tirade, and noticing the battle wounds on her arms, the nice woman doctor suggested that the psychiatrist could recommend a medication. Of course this was the woman doctor's way of getting her there, and it worked to some degree. The woman doctor probably pictured the psychiatrist talking to her, relieving the symptoms that seemed to plague her mental state. The woman doctor probably pictured an honest doctor who wouldn't just write out a prescription and hand it over after five minutes of conversation. The woman doctor probably didn't imagine the return visits in which other medications were prescribed to relieve the symptoms that the previous medications caused.

Ashley got back in the car, drove over bridges, under bridges, around them, as if there'd never been a problem. Still, she watched no television, read no newspapers, only responded to the list of illnesses she believed afflicted her. She visited the old doctor who stooped when he walked; he too prescribed medications to alleviate the pain that she felt in her back from what she thought was scoliosis, to relieve her chronic fatigue syndrome, to relieve her mitral-valve prolapse.

The Thinker

I attempt days and abandon them, too much like the low hanging sky. I lie on the couch for hours, not hungry, not thirsty, uselessly wrangling air in and out of my nostrils.

My chest feels heavy, my breathing constricted, as if a pressure slowly descends down upon me much like a woman being stoned to death; as if someone is slowly placing large bricks and rocks on my chest, robbing me of air, for some imagined wrong done to a town or to a person. I imagine for a while that they are relieving me of life.

I worry endlessly. The anxiety that trapped my sister indoors for a year and the compulsivity that forced her to climb ladders and scrub ceilings, that kept my other sister from moving vehicles and bridges, manifests itself in my concern. I worry about low flying planes, cancer-causing cell phones, the bovine growth hormone in milk, estrogen, the baseboards in the bathroom, black mold, money I spent last month, last week, last year, next year, taxes, bugs, gophers. I worry about the loose seal around the refrigerator door letting out energy, not keeping food cold enough, letting bugs in, and I worry about the constancy of spiders.

I don't sleep nights. I toss, turn, and dream strange dreams about big, red houses with big, red doors, and little white cloud girls being attacked by big, red Bengals. I stay up in the wee hours, making love to the darkness, the silence, the aloneness of the empty nights. Sometimes I write many words on many pieces of paper and abandon those too. I try to imagine where we all began and where we will all end. Sometimes I walk the empty midnight streets alone; once, it was with my sisters. It was a time we could go out, a time we could be alone in the darkness of the dank and empty streets. The night is a safe place, a comforting place for us, a time to be together, and the world to be gone. And I think if that were our lives, much like this night, we could all be happy.

That Night

It was a washed over day, clouds the color of dirty dish water descended down upon us, made me feel tired, dreary, made us want to abandon all hope and commit ourselves to lesser non-pursuits, napping, television-watching, wall-monitoring.

The night came and relieved us from our daytime depressions and we walked the midnight streets.

A lovely soft rain fell down on our faces, our shoulders.

We believed we had a curse upon us, an evil spirit, something shadowed us, pulled strings, did things to keep us in a drippy daytime darkness that didn't let us breathe or live a normal life. The night was different.

A Substitute

My father's boss was the most beautiful man I'd ever seen: tall with shining blue eyes and white hair that saw fit only to adorn the sides above the ears and around the back of his head, like a partial halo. He wore a dress shirt, blue, with black pants, black shiny shoes that never seemed to smudge. His office seemed to be the headquarters of his life, big oak bookcases, a great oak desk, and lots of things children could look at, but not touch. He smoked a fancy red and brown pipe with designs carved deep into it and, when he lit it, the room filled with thick cherry smoke.

My father's boss lived on a ranch far from the city and, once in a while, on a summer day, we were invited to a barbeque or picnic there. We'd eat and then the women would adjourn to the kitchen to clean up and chat and the men, or more clearly, my father and his boss made their way down the eleven steps to his office. The children were free to roam the fields, pick wildflowers, hunt for a four-leafed clover, or even lie under a tree and watch the soft sky-cotton float by in the forms of bunnies, angels, and fairies. I always made my way downstairs to that office to hear the men talk. They talked about work, business, people, and things I'd never understand.

My dad's boss's wife - a Japanese woman who knew enough English to hold a conversation with my mother but not to understand the men's business talk. I think he chose Kumiko, not for her flat-faced Asian beauty, but for the way she served him, waited on him, and for her gift of foresight. She knew before he asked if he needed a drink, an ashtray, or the like. He'd joke about her Japanese temper, but we'd never seen it.

Then came time for the children to leave the office, for the men to talk. They talked about other types of business, about women in a way Mother wouldn't have liked me to hear. I heard Father once tell Mother his boss always "kept a little on the side." I thought he meant money, or something secret and wonderful and golden, but I heard my mother tell someone he kept a girl. I thought they meant a little girl and wished, for a moment, it could be me, but then that didn't feel quite right.

Then the children left the kitchen so the women could have their talk, which included sad faces and surprise "ohs' and hushed "ahs" and sometimes didn't. We were relegated to the yards, the patios, or the TV room.

Sometimes I liked going there. The large green world all around us, the smell of smoke, grass, dirt. Our little place had none of these things. But I didn't like the evenings, when the women sipped their kitchen wine, the men clinked ice cubes covered in thick yellow liquids in short glasses. Everyone became too serious, too quiet, and no one left happy. Sometimes I thought how lucky to have been the child of my father's boss. And sometimes not.

Chloe and the Rock Star

She started dating. She'd met a construction worker with a nice body and a golden head of locks that we all knew Chloe loved. He asked her to meet his family.

"Uhm, could you wear make-up?"

She put on make-up she hadn't worn in two years, put on nice clothes, newly purchased. They arrived for dinner and his family was pleasant, if not warm. It was clear they would not interfere with a relationship. It was clear that Rick was on his own and made his own decisions and the family had little to say in or about his life.

He wanted her to meet his friends.

"Could you wear shorts?"

Shorts wouldn't be a problem, if she didn't feel out of place among these men in their jeans and their wives in assorted outfits. But he had said she had good legs and wanted her to show them off and it was a compliment that she would have been happy to fulfill.

He wanted to spend the night at her place.

"Could you make me some breakfast already?" He laid in bed and rolled over; he would have to leave for work in an hour or so and they had talked about breakfast in passing, but she saw it as a romantic thing that they would do together, making pancakes and potatoes, but she knew he was tired and had to work and so she didn't mind getting up and taking care of him. It felt sort of nice, having someone to do things for.

He wanted to move in with her.

"Can you clean this place up once in a while?" His tone wasn't amusing to her. But she knew she had fallen off on her scrubbing since the doctor prescribed the Prozac. So, although she didn't like his tone, she did agree that the house needed straightening and cleaning. And that day she brought the stepladder up again and started in the bedroom, since that is where they spent the most time. But when he got home, he said he had meant the bathroom; all her hair stuff and lotions and make up and everything was in his way, couldn't she put it in a cabinet somewhere out of sight?

So the following day she rearranged the bathroom and put her things in her bedroom, some on her dresser with the mirror and some in the top drawer; she arranged it nicely with a dresser scarf made some years before by her great grandmother before she had died. His dresser was on the opposite wall and was adorned with his things, cologne and the like.

Rick liked the bathroom, but did not like the bedroom. He opened her top dresser drawer and swiped everything into it. "I like this better. I'm tired of this place looking so feminine."

It was her place, she reminded him. He turned without a word and left for the night.

She called and called and found him at a bar a few blocks over. She walked over to find him having a beer with a few friends. He didn't say anything, just asked her if she wanted a beer and then ordered one for her even though she wasn't allowed to drink on the medication. Soon, feeling things were okay, she went home expecting he would be along soon. But he wasn't.

At 5am, an hour before he had to go to work, drunk and stinking and strange, he woke her up by playing with her hair. When she asked him what he was doing, he slapped her and laughed. She called him an ass and turned away.

He didn't go to work that day, nor the next. He did go out that night and the next. He came home strange and angry. In the wee hours of the morning, she woke up to pee and stumbled toward the bathroom. He was not in bed, but that wasn't unusual anymore and so she didn't worry and refused to let it bother her until the real daylight hours. She made her way through the house-darkness and opened the bathroom door. Rick sat on the closed toilet with a belt around his arm and a needle in his hand.

"What the hell are you doing?" They both yelled at the same time.

He leapt at her and grabbed her by the hair. He threatened to stick the needle into her neck.

"I'll put an air bubble in your vein and watch it go to your heart and kill you."

She could see herself in the mirror. She could see him in the mirror. Her face was red, frightened, disfigured in the night light of the bathroom blue. His was almost angelic, the mane of lovely blonde hair surrounding his face, the pallid skin and the glow about him. He didn't even look angry. He saw her looking at their reflection in the mirror and he studied it for a moment, laughed and let her go.

"I'm just kidding baby, I swear. When you first came in, I didn't know who it was. I'm so tired. I'm just messing with you though. Right? You know that, right? I love you. You are my heart song." He petted her and kissed her gently on her cheeks and mouth.

He wanted to make love and so they did, or tried. He couldn't stay hard, fell asleep. In the bright hours of the morning, he got up, thinking she was still asleep; he went into her purse that sat on her dresser, took the last of the money that she had and before she could roll out of bed to ask him where he was going, he was gone. She thought he might be going out to get some breakfast, but he didn't come back that day. He came back the next.

"I'm not going to take this." She stood up to him in the freshly cleaned kitchen. "I won't live with someone who does drugs and treats me like this." And she was proud of herself.

"I understand, Baby. But will you give me a chance? A chance to clean up my act and show you how much I love you?"

She nodded hesitantly. Those were the words she wanted to hear, but they came quickly and easily without a fight, without hesitation and, maybe, just maybe, this meant that things were going to be okay.

He spent the day with her, making lunch and taking a bath, making love and settling in front of the television for a romantic movie. They fell asleep in each other's arms and she knew that was what love was supposed to be about. She watched him sleep, those lovely blonde curls resting on her shoulder, the soft breath in and out and it comforted her into a deep sleep where she dreamed of the African plain and a Lion family playing in the grass and amongst the trees. When it was time to eat, it was the lioness, the lioness she felt was the image of her, that hunted and killed the deer and brought it back for the family to eat.

But when the lioness woke up in the morning, when Chloe woke up in the morning, her mate was gone. And so were the pills that her doctor prescribed. And the pearl earrings that her grandmother had given her.

She cried and allowed herself her own little fit. She went into the bathroom and tossed his assorted bottles of cologne and aftershave around, breaking them. A large piece of glass, the corner of the colored greenish bottle, had lodged itself upright into the floor and Chloe sat on the edge of the tub studying it. She thought of suicide. She thought about stepping on it hard, forcing her foot onto it and hoping to cut that artery that would bring her to a strange and wonderful death. She imagined herself walking around with the blood gushing out of her foot; she could make herself tea and toast and sit on the couch to watch the blood gush. She turned and looked deep into the bleached white porcelain of the bathtub. She could fill it with bubbly hot water and lie there until she fell asleep; she would imagine that there would be some controversy as to whether it was an accident or planned. But then, she had another idea.

She stepped carelessly over the glass and went and got his clothes, everything he owned from his dresser and took them to the living room and slowly and methodically cut them into long strips. She arranged them in piles according to color and then, beginning at the back door, where he might, when he came back, come through, she laid the strips in the form of a walkway to the living room. At first she took the reds and laid them out, then yellows, whites and beiges, but then she stopped. She didn't like that look. She went back and started over, laying the strips of fabric so they resembled a variegated stone walkway. Some red strips, some white/beige/yellow, and then outlined in the darker colors. This she liked much better. But there were his nice pale blue dress shirts that didn't really fit into her walkway. For those, she went into the basement and found the wallpaper glue she had seen down there from her cleaning trips. On the wall, with the strips of silk articulately placed, she wrote: "Rick – The Rock Star."

Ashley and the Alien

Her best girlfriend was Tiffany, a pretty girl who arrived soon after Ashley's reappearance. Tiffany had battle wounds of all kinds, most of them fresh and full at any given time. Tiffany had two children who lived with her mother; Social Services had deemed her to be an unfit parent and put them up for adoption. Their grandmother, feeling a responsibility, took them in and tried hard to redo her life as a working single parent with young children and little help. Tiffany, at that time, was pregnant again. She planned to marry the father with whom she lived on W. 43rd in a nice little duplex in an old, but once grand neighborhood. Ashley spent much time over there with them, days, nights, weeks.

When Tiffany went into labor, her boyfriend said he had business and left her alone in the house. Ashley used Grandmother's car to go pick her up and take her to the hospital. Ashley stayed with her and went into the delivery room with her. She watched the baby being born; she caught the baby and, later, said it was the best moment in her life.

"What is it?" Tiffany asked when the last labor pain subsided and she could speak again.

"It looks like an alien." Ashley laughed and let the doctor take the baby, clean it, and wrap a blanket around it.

"I want to name her Skye." Tiffany closed her eyes and tried to relax.

The doctor came over and handed her the baby. "You have a son."

"A son." Tiffany opened her eyes long enough to take the baby. "Ashley could you take him?" Ashley took the bundle wrapped in blue and looked at his big face and little eyes and pursing lips. "Skye, tell them Skye is his name." And Tiffany fell asleep before the afterbirth finished its journey.

The nurses passed looks between them and asked if they should feed him formula. Ashley shrugged, attempted to ask Tiffany who waved her away, and said "sure." Ashley sat in the birthing room feeding Skye as Tiffany slept. Then she put him in his little hospital approved baby bed and secured the swaddling cloth and fell asleep on the chair, waiting. When the baby cried, Tiffany still slept, and it was Ashley who tended to him, who answered the nurses' questions, who called the respective grandmas and tried to find the baby's daddy to let him know he had a son. And it was Ashley who drove them home, picked up the diapers and baby formula, reminded Tiffany that she'd already named him Skye and couldn't change it to Alan after the baby's father.

Alan, the father, reappeared a day or so later, smiled at the little boy, cooed at him until the boy started crying for his mother or for food, both of which Ashley took care of as Tiffany was sleeping.

Whether Tiffany was awake or asleep, whether Tiffany or Alan were there or not, it was Ashley who joyfully took care of Skye. She took him for long walks in the fresh air, tending to his booties, setting the stroller's shade against the haze, and corrected the old woman of the neighborhood who congratulated her. She woke to give him his 2 a.m. feeding and his 4 a.m. feeding if he still woke for it. She bathed him and dressed him and even shopped for the clothes he wore. Tiffany liked having him around. She played with him. Occasionally fed him, but when he started crying or when she got bored, she didn't know what else to do. And when she wanted to go out, she went.

Although the war was all around her, with Alan and Tiffany acting as Generals, Ashley's battle wounds subsided and began to heal. She thought more about taking care of the baby than she did about herself. When she didn't think about herself, she didn't need it, nor the meds the doctor prescribed, which was good since Alan had taken those along time ago.

One day, upon returning from the grocery store, Ashley could hear the baby cry from the bottom of the stairs. She called for Tiffany and for Alan, but no one answered. She went upstairs to find the baby alone, wet, cold and crying.

In the same bright and early daylight, a knock came at the door. Ashley stumbled down the stairs, thinking they had forgotten their keys. When she answered the door, the tall, lovely black woman with purple eye shadow that matched her suit jacket identified herself as being from Social Services and looking for Tiffany Swan who'd just had another baby.

"I'm sure you have the wrong address." Ashley had become a master at minute stories. "I just moved in, but I've never heard of that person."

"So, there are no children here?"

"No. Well, not usually. I do baby-sit once in a while."

The lovely black woman with the purple eye shadow looked skeptical. "I'll have to check with the office."

She walked back to her car, pulled paperwork out of her briefcase, and called into the office, then sat there and waited. Ashley dressed Skye, slipped out the back door, into the alley, and around the corner to a busy store from which she called her grandmother for a ride.

She called Tiffany's mother, dialed all of Tiffany's and Alan's friends; no one had seen them but would give them the message if they did. For three days, she could not reach them; for three days, no one had seen them. One night in a hazy rain, there came a pounding at her mother's door where she'd flown with the baby.

"It's Tiffany," the voice yelled.

"Where have you been?" Ashley unlocked the deadbolt and the door flew open on her, a gun pushed into her face.

"You took my baby!" Tiffany screamed. "Where is she?"

Ashley looked at her in disbelief as Alan pushed her in and shut the door behind them. "HE is in the bassinette there."

"You took my drugs." Alan put the gun to her head.

"No, I didn't."

"We came back and the police were there. They were looking for our baby." Tiffany picked up the baby who started crying. "This is not Alan Jr."

"Yes, it is." Ashley knew they must be hurting, in need of the drugs they thought she had.

"Social services came. They wanted the baby. I brought him here so they couldn't take him."

"You called the cops." Alan pushed the gun into her neck.

"Will you stop it!" She'd seen them like this before. He'd go off like this, but so far had never hurt her or Tiffany.

"No, stupid, if they knew you were there and they were looking for the baby, the social services woman probably called them and they probably have your drugs. I told you to hide them."

"Who you callin' stupid?" He smacked the side of her head with the gun. "This is your fault." He pointed the gun across the room toward Tiffany and the baby. You had to have that little bastard."

"He's not a bastard. He's your son."

"I ought to fuckin' kill all of you and leave the fuckin' cops to find your worthless corpses."

"Shut the fuck up," Tiffany yelled back.

Their voices rose as they argued back and forth about the baby, the drugs, the gun. Ashley's mother awoke upstairs. The neighbor's lights flipped on and then off again.

They knew they'd overstayed their welcome.

"Leave the baby here for now," Ashley begged as Tiffany pushed passed her. She knew the baby would not be safe with them, would not be cared for with Tiffany. "I'll take him to your mom's."

"Fuck my mom. Like I want her taking care of my kids."

"I'll take care of him then."

"No, you're trying to turn him against me," Tiffany started crying. "You're trying to take my baby away and make him hate me."

The sounds of sirens in the distance ushered them out the door, with the baby, with the gun, with threats of returning if they didn't find their drugs.

The police came and Ashley told them some truths.

Tiffany's mother told them the rest when they went to talk to her.

Ashley spent many hours at Tiffany's mother's place after that, looking after the other kids, but it wasn't the same and she started feeling that need again.

The Cloud People

Honey, those fluffy pillow forms that dot the sky are cloud children. From the big clouds, little ones break away; white cottony figures float across the sky. They run and play and change shapes. They can look like just about anything, a frog, a rabbit, a flower. They change shapes to hide; they don't want their parents to call them home too early. But far across the blue seas where the earth meets the sky, the parents catch up with the children and, as the sun sets, they go home with their families.

The Vampire

     I live in the dark. I take night classes and work night jobs and don't date and don't have friends. I stay up until two or three each morning, writing words on papers and organizing them into files. I listen to Pete Townshend tell tall tales of sweet ennui. I listen to the crickets in the spring, the cicadas in the summer, and the birds in the fall. I watch the lightning bugs hover over greening grass after the rain and before the sun, if, indeed, there ever is a sun.

     The family believes I am happy. They think I am living a life, even more of a life than my two sisters, an even better life than my two sisters. I am not on medication. I am not in therapy. I am not taking drugs. I am not hanging out with losers.

     When I sleep, I dream I'm somewhere far away on a warm and sunny coast; the sound of waves rushing play in the background as soft sand works its way between my toes. Pete Townshend is there and he won't talk to me.

Melanie; Forget Me Not

We hated when Mother would go out. She didn't
drive so she walked to the bar down the street. We
would cry and hold onto her thighs and ask her please
not to go. But she would go, not because she needed the
drink but because she needed to get out and be an adult.
In any case, we didn't like it. We tried to stay awake
until we could see her walk back up the street, her breath
bruming in the cool night air, creating a mist around her
face, head, and trailing behind her, or until we heard the
backdoor open and close with the stomp of her shoes on
the floor as she wiped the dirt or rain or snow from her
feet. Little Red always fell asleep first, and sometimes
Chloe next, but I always stayed awake. Even long after
she was home, I laid in bed and listened to the adults
talk about grown up things that I was not supposed to
understand. Their voices were different at night. They

were calmer, slower, lighter, and filled with something that was not there when we were.

Man of the Clouds

A cool fall wind had blown in; the leaves, brilliant red and gold, blew past our windows, past our doors, gathered in corners of the porch, of the yard, the streets. It was early morning, before the storm moved in. We laid our baby faces against the cold pane of glass and blew clouds of foggy breath onto the window. We tried to spell good-bye but didn't know how, so we drew hearts and spelled out "hi" in the middle with our fingers. Our faces dirtied, our fingertips blackened, we tried to see through our temporary and fading art to the street where our father stood with our mother. Mother followed behind him hurriedly; her thin nightgown and slippers under her winter coat. We watched the scene from our upstairs bedroom window, knocking, calling, nudging each other out of the way for a better view.

The Days

The clouds never seemed to lift; gray formless, creaseless clouds followed us, hung over our heads, creating those lonely languid days that left us in hopelessness hell. In the days after Dad disappeared, the spring drew on longer and darker than ever. April showers began in February and lasted until June gloom took over the heated summer sadness; then came August with the fatal threat of school hanging a noose around our necks dragging us to a certain end.

It was the year that we didn't celebrate Valentine's Day, nor St. Patrick's Day, nor Easter. The anniversary of Bunny hopping/Jesus rising was spent looking out the window hoping, searching, praying for our father to appear. It was the time of miracles, we'd learned so many years ago in Vacation Bible School, and so we dared to let ourselves believe that on this day the thick and deathly sallow heavens would crack and the sun would come through with rays of colors to illuminate our lives. But it never happened. The sky grew darker, the stratus thicker, and it rained harder throughout the day until the night rushed in black and quiet. We slept on the floor together in the damp coolness to the sounds of Charlton Heston breaking the stone tablets over the non-believers.

Chloe and the Medicine Man

     In order for her disability insurance to continue, Chloe had to stay on the medication and to see the psychologist regularly. She began with telephone appointments; her anxiety still too strong for her to go out. Once the medication kicked in, she felt a little better but still had trouble with loud or crowded places. The mall and the supermarket were off limits. She did make it to the corner store and out for an occasional walk with her mother.

     The psychologist wanted to put her on another medication, or an additional medication to help with the fear of crowds, but she wouldn't go for it. She did let him change her medication, but then called him in a panic, certain her heart was beating too slowly and saying she was about to pass out. Against her wishes, he sent an ambulance, thinking it was a real medical emergency. She did let them in, did let them take her stats but refused to go outside and get into the ambulance to be taken to the hospital. The doctor immediately changed her prescription back to what it used to be. She refused to try anything new again.

There came a time when the psychologist, Dr. Bruce, wanted her to come in to the office. She said she'd try. Her grandmother drove her and waited outside in the car. Because of Chloe's condition, the doctor took her in the second she walked through the door and said he was glad he had gotten a chance to meet face to face; did she think she could make it to the office now for regular visits because disability would want to see she was making progress? She thought he was flirting with her; she liked it, so she said yes. She'd come every Wednesday at one o'clock, "that would not be a problem."

When she left the session, she was starry eyed, happier than she'd felt months, excited, talking non-stop to her grandmother who'd waited, then to her mother whom they stopped by to see on the way home. She was certain it was love at first sight, or accepted that it might be lust, but she'd made up her mind at that moment that she would have Dr. Bruce.

Each Wednesday at one p.m., she would go to his office, always having taken the whole morning to get ready, do her hair, her make up, and change clothes no less than a dozen times. She'd even ventured out to buy new clothes for some of the visits. She wanted him to notice her, and he did.

"You are looking well today. How are you feeling?"

"I'm feeling well, and you are looking wonderful."

He'd chuckle and say, "Thank you; you're too kind." And they would begin their session. He not only wanted to know from what source this anxiety stemmed; he wanted her to get well and live a normal life. She, however, had no desire to dredge up the past and find what forgotten horrors might lie there. She'd had some hard times, she'd say. But she was certain this anxiety was caused by a chemical imbalance as the medical doctor told her. Because she had no desire to get well enough to stop seeing Dr. Bruce, sometimes she made up stories, panic attack stories.

She'd kept her appointments with him for a good six months, and she was looking for a job, at his urging. She felt, finally, excited about life, about possibilities. Chloe had a plan, she confessed to him one day.

"When I have this job," (she was pretty sure she'd get a secretarial job she'd just interviewed for), "I think we need to stop these sessions."

"Really, why?"

"Well, I'm doing much better, no anxiety and, if I have problems, you can recommend someone."

"Have you become uncomfortable with me?" His manner, comforting and reassuring as usual.

"Oh, no, I just don't think I should be coming to you for therapy if we are dating." She smiled thinking she was being rather cute and coy.

"I'm sorry?" He wanted to make certain he'd heard correctly. "Chloe, of course I'm fond of you and we have formed a bond in this room that cannot be taken anywhere outside of this room. It would be unprofessional of me to date any of my patients and I could lose my license." Certainly he kicked himself for not seeing this sooner.

"What do you mean? But you were flirting with me, telling me how good I looked."

"I attempted to reassure you that you were improving and you've been doing wonderfully. This is quite natural for patients to become attached to their doctors, so I don't want you to be embarrassed."

It was too late; she was embarrassed and angry. He had been flirting with her, she believed. He'd lead her on and now, now!, he worried about losing his license! She said nothing but turned her eyes downward.

"I think at this point, I should recommend another psychologist for you. How do you feel about that?"

"Sure." Not that she planned on going.

He left the room to get a phone number, probably to take a deep breath of fresh air. She stood up, walked around the office, behind his desk, and picked up her file. In his handwriting, on the first page, "OCD, signs of anxiety, fear of crowds, agoraphobic, altophobic, possibly verminophobic…given to panic attacks… displays of dramatics…" It went on and on and on. At that point, he walked back into the room.

"I am not obsessive compulsive." She threw the file at his feet. "I do not have all these things. You are a liar. You led me on all these months and you know it! Do you flirt with all your female patients to make yourself feel better? I'd like to see what your file says. Probably insecurity issues, must lie to women." She stormed out, through the reception room and down the hall breaking into tears in the elevator and not speaking a word when she got into the car with her waiting grandmother.

She did get the job. She wasn't going to take it, but disability had cut her off since she refused to see any more psychologists. The stooped, old, medical doctor still gave her prescriptions, Prozac for the anxiety, Xanax for the side effects and, occasionally, others if she complained.

The Matriarch

Grandma and our father did not get along. She didn't come to visit when he was there. We went to visit her. I remember her orange shag carpet and the matching striped polyester pantsuits she made for us. My mom's hair was cut into a bob, and mine and the sisters were cut under bowls because, as Grandma said, "you are not old enough to care for it and your mother doesn't have the time to take care of it for you."

When she came to visit us, it was after our father had disappeared. And she didn't leave. We were required to "do things for yourself, your mother does not have time to do it for you." So we learned to brush our hair and tie our shoes and Little Red was spanked until she learned to pee in the potty instead of in her diaper or in our bed.

In the middle of one night, I woke wet and cold. I toddled to my mother's bed and pushed and poked but she would not wake. Because I was old enough, I changed my underwear, put a towel on the spot and fell back asleep. In the dreary morning light, Grandma lined us up in the kitchen next to the green Formica table and ordered us to tell who had done it. But I could not, as scared of her as I was, I could not open my mouth and neither of the sisters spoke either.

In our room for the next week we stayed, alone and without toys or television to entertain us. We spoke and played quietly. Little red haired Ashley did not understand and kept at the door crying and we tried to hush her and tell her stories lest we bring Grandma to the other side of the door. I told Chloe that it had been me, and that I was too afraid to say. She said she knew and she didn't care because she didn't like Grandma or the nicknames she gave us.

It was she who called Ashley Little Red and she who nicknamed Chloe Sleeping Beauty and it was she who said I had no name yet. She said maybe Cinderella, but I certainly didn't do enough work and no man would ever come and get me if I didn't do my share of work.

Grandma did buy us things. She said she was there to make Christmas nice for us, because "children should always have gifts at Christmas, even if they didn't appreciate them later." She gave me a Cinderella hair dryer that was much like a grown up dryer with a hose that went to a hat and covered the top of my head. She said I needed to keep my hair nice because that's what nice girls did.

Grandma was sick a lot. Not the kind of sickness that sent her to the hospital or to bed with chicken soup and cherry flavored medicine. The kind that kept her from Bingo and made her limp because her "sciatica was acting up." And the kind that kept her from climbing the stairs because she "can't breathe with this shortness of breath." She'd sit on the couch and yell out for our mother.

"Mel, come here. Bring me my pills."

"Which ones?"

"I don't know. The ones in the big bottle that the doctor just gave me. And bring me a cup of coffee, I can't swallow those damn things."

The Cloud People

Sometimes clouds get sad. When they get sad they start to sink, and sink, and sink. Sometimes they get caught up there, on the very topmost part of the mountains, and sometimes they slip down even further and they come to rest here on the streets around the houses, schools, and stores. No one is certain why the clouds get sad. Perhaps they are just lonely for their earth siblings and they come to visit. If the children go out to play, the sad cloud will want to stay. Children must stay in and play on those days so the cloud knows it must go home.

Melanie and The Treasure Chest

     Mel, as my Grandmother called her, had a secret box in her dresser that the sisters and I found upon playing where we shouldn't have been playing. It was a brown box with flowers pressed into its smoothed acrylic surface. The top was rounded and opened like a treasure chest. We expected to find gold, jewels, treasures that could make us rich, that could keep us from eating peanut butter sandwiches every day, that would afford Chloe ballet shoes she had seen in a book, that might get us a car of our very own so Grandma didn't have to live here. But when we opened it, there were only letters, little trinkets that might have once been pieces to an old charm bracelet, and a package of sweet cherry smelling paper shreds that reminded me of Dad's boss's lovely brown pipe. I stuck my face in and sucked such a big breath that I started coughing and choking. Our mother came in to see what the matter was and started yelling and took the treasure box away from us. Later, when I came to apologize, I saw her crying over the box. I thought we had broken something, ruined it somehow. I hugged her big waist with my little arms and cried.

"I'm sorry I broke it." I sobbed. "It's all my fault cuz I'm the oldest and I should know better."

She rubbed my back and told me that it wasn't the treasure box that was broken. Then she said for me to please go play and keep the sisters out of trouble.

t Night

Ashley snuck off into the parking lot across from the old Wonderbread outlet store. A car drove by, a car full of men that wolf whistled and drove away. Chloe flirted, waving to the men. The street was quiet, wet, dark, cool. Our jackets nestled around our necks, we watched our breath billow, crystallize and then dissipate, gone in the night. Laughing, Ashley climbed up onto a Silver Dodge Ram and kicked at the hood ornament until it came loose. She jumped up and down, pounding on her chest, a mock King Kong, and jumped down once again out of our sight. The car drove around again. The men called out, would we like a ride? Chloe smiled and waved. I grabbed her hand down, called Ashley to come out of the darkness of the parking lot, and we turned toward home.

Chloe and the Phone man

When we were playing children, Chloe once said she heard a phone call. She overheard something on the phone. Something about a little woman on the side. Something that my mother told to someone. Something else that my grandmother had told to someone else. She wasn't sure. But she remembered the phone. She remembered the woman. She knew she lived on the West End. And she thought that was where we could find father.

Other Alien Forms

As young children, before we had come to understand the night, it was dark and strange sometimes. Out the chilled window, the city was so quiet one night, it allowed us to wake to the sounds of hushed voices. In the dark kitchen with the light over the stove doing its best to splash onto the table, he talked to our mother. From the bedroom, where bugs made trails under the door and we rarely ventured out, we heard agitated whispers.

When we dared toddle, whining and frightened, into the splash of light, we became the argument. The man from the shadow with the octopus arms grabbed us and spanked us on our naked baby fatted legs with big calloused open hands and threw us into bed; sobbing and scared, we clung to each other.

When I told this dream to Chloe, she said it wasn't an REM sleep that had brought this on. That octopus had been our father the night before the day he disappeared.

When I told this dream to Ashley, she said it symbolized a small child's fear of the unknown. The octopus was the fear the day after our father disappeared. And she thinks Chloe makes things up.

Man of the Clouds

I remember his smiling face looking down at me, tickling me, making me laugh and smile. I remember the sound of my own giggle in response to his songs.

The Cloud People

They like to keep things very clean. After the parties are over, and the cloud children have laid down to rest, the cloud parents clean. They wash their cloud dishes and they wash their cloud clothes and they wash their cloud floors and when they pour the water on the floor to scrub, some of it drains down through the clouds and it cleans the sky and falls down on the earth and cleans the earth.

Melanie and the Man with the Money

When we were old enough to play outside by ourselves, we did. That was when the sun still shined. We were digging a hole to China because we wanted to have a short cut to the other side of the world where our mother said The Chinaman lived. The neighbor lady came out to empty her garbage and looked over the fence.

"What are you kids doing there?"

"Digging a hole to China," we answered.

"Ah," she laughed. "Well, if you strike water, you know you're close. Now you be careful not to fall in."

We got as deep as rusted pipes and suddenly feared that we would fall in and never get back. We hurriedly covered the hole, kicking the dirt from a safe distance. Our once pink and white play clothes now brown and yellowed, our hands rough and dirtied, our shoes filled, we ran into the house.

"Mommy, we need a bath."

The man who smoked the cherry smelling pipe and talked business for long hours with our father in his basement office handed her some money and kissed her cheek. She wiped her face, I thought she was wiping away the kiss, but when she turned toward me and said "wait just a minute, hon," her eyes shined the way Little Red's always did when she cried.

We waited in the bathroom, taking our shoes off, and then our clothes. When she came in she didn't say anything, but ran our bath and sat there watching us.

"Was the man looking for Daddy?"

She looked at me for a long time, then nodded. "Yes, he was."

That Night

The night grew more ominous, for the first time since we had made friends with it. The streetlights dimmed and failed to work. The moon securely hidden behind the clouds, we made our way home. The sisters did not want to go. They wanted to play at the midnight park. They wanted to talk to strangers in cars. They were angry with me for bringing them home. I lay in my bed listening to the wind tiptoe around the house, making its way in through the cracks and down the halls. The house creaked and shivered, the trees thumped against the side of the house and I fell into a deep sleep.

Sometime later, the sisters knocked on my window, holding themselves against the wind. I opened the curtains and pushed on the frame until it gave.

"You got to take us to the emergency room," Chloe cried.

"I think we're dying. I feel like I'm coming out of my body." Ashley wrapped her arms around herself.

"Hold on to me, I think I'm coming out of my body."
And she wrapped her arms around Chloe.

"What happened?" I grabbed for jeans and put them on over my pajamas.

"Don't tell Mom or Grandma. Just meet us out back with the keys."

"What happened? What did you do?"

"We went out with those guys; we smoked something."

"What did you smoke?"

"Come on, just hurry. We have to go to the doctor's." They headed for the back, slinking passed Mother's bedroom window and into the backyard.

Grandma was asleep on the couch with the television singing holiday carols to her.

I took the keys from the hook and locked the back door behind me.

The Cloud People

Long ago, people were clouds. But families sometimes move, and the children grow up and there's a big, vast emptiness. There aren't many families left in those clouds, so sometimes all that can be heard are faint echoes. But when the sky grows bleak with thick dark clouds and they begin to rumble and vibrate and the sound thrums through children's ears, it's nothing to be afraid of, you must listen hard for the laughter.

Little Red and The Man Who Knew Too Little

The stooped old doctor gave Ashley more prescriptions. But the Xanax blurred her vision and gave her migraines until the fear of aneurisms filled her once again. The Prozac gave her night terrors and heart palpitations until she thought that her chest was going to burst. And the Doxepin caused such a dramatic weight loss that she looked like the decaying dead. She stopped taking them and sought out the nice woman doctor. She wanted someone else, another psychiatrist who wouldn't push her off with medications in hand. She wanted to talk to someone, to find out why she was the way she was. She wanted someone to stop the feelings of fear and hopelessness that overwhelmed her every day and kept her from sleeping or dreaming. But the next psychiatrist said he couldn't help her unless she agreed to take the medication, and only then would he make regular appointments with her. The psychiatrist after that said he would use medication and behavior modification, but she would have to stay on the medicines or he wouldn't work with her. The next one referred her to a psychologist. And she sat on his big brown leather chair, not feeling comfortable, not feeling the desire to be there, ready to run out of the room the moment he mentioned any medication; Prozac, priolec, effexor. She couldn't take another round of anything.

"I'm not taking medicines of any kind," she said before he even spoke.

"Oh, okay, what kind of medicines do you not want to take?"

"Any kind. I'm not doing it. They all make me sick. I just don't want to do that. I want to be normal again."

"What seems to be the problem?"

"I have a fear of bridges." She looked at him to see if he was going to laugh as the last guy did. He didn't. "And sometimes I can't get into cars."

"Motion sickness?"

She shrugged, playing with her fingers, with strings from her jacket. "And sometimes it feels like I can't breathe, like I'm trying too and I can't get enough air in my lungs. I'm pretty sure that I have mitral-valve prolapse."

"Did you have that checked out?"

She nodded without looking up. "Everyday, I wake up and I just think I'm going to die."

"Someday, you'll be right."

She stopped playing with her fingers, her jacket; she stopped her nervous fidgeting and looked at him. He had come around his desk and sat on the edge; his face broke into a smile. And the strain on her face disappeared into a half hopeful grin.

"So where do you think we ought to begin?" He asked her.

She shrugged, still looking at him. "Where do people usually begin?"

"At the beginning." He took the seat across from her and leaned forward to listen.

The Lost

Grandma assures me that we will all be all right, if we just get married and have kids. "That's it," she says. "You just have to pull yourself off of that couch and go out there and find yourself a man."

But the gray drippy sky keeps me here, longing for the days to end.

Man of the Clouds

Father said it would end. The rain would stop,
the clouds will part, and the blue sky will show through.
He said all you had to do was wait and see.
So, I'm waiting.

Also by Noreen Lace:

West End

Here in the Silence

Dad Shining

Follow Noreen Lace:

www.NoreenLace.com